For Phoebe Anabel Jones – A.G.

For Molly, always my inspiration – S.McN.

First published in the United States 2004
by Dial Books for Young Readers
A division of Penguin Young Readers Group
345 Hudson Street
New York, New York 10014

Published in Great Britain by Orchard Books
Text copyright © 2003 by Adèle Geras
Illustrations copyright © 2003 by Shelagh McNicholas
Text set in Stempel Schneidler
Manufactured in Singapore
1 3 5 7 9 10 8 6 4 2

Library of Congress Cataloging-in-Publication Data
Geras, Adèle
Time for ballet / by Adèle Geras ; illustrated by Shelagh McNicholas.
p. cm.
Summary: Tilly, who loves ballet, plays the part of a cat in her class's dance recital.
ISBN 0-8037-2978-2
[1. Ballet dancing—Fiction. 2. Dance recitals—Fiction.]
I. McNicholas, Shelagh, ill. II. Title.
PZ7.G29354Ti 2004
[E]—dc21 2003005751

Time for Ballet

by *Adèle Geras* ❖ illustrated by *Shelagh McNicholas*

DIAL BOOKS FOR YOUNG READERS ▲ NEW YORK

It's Tuesday. It's ballet class day!
My favorite day of the week.
Mom calls me Tutu Tilly because
I love ballet so much.

At the dance studio, we all put on
our special ballet clothes.
I have a pretty pink leotard
and tutu to wear.

Katie's leotard
is purple.

Ballet clothes aren't very easy to get into.

Miss Anne, our teacher, claps her hands to start the class. This is the last lesson before our big show, so we must all practice extra hard.

We do warm-up exercises first.
Katie likes

"happy back,

grumpy back"

because she's good
at that, but I like

"good toes,

naughty toes."

Sometimes my toes get
a bit mixed up, but
Miss Anne says I'll be
all right if I just slow
down a little.

Next we go through our positions:

first,

second,

third,

fourth,

and fifth.

Then we practice our
curtsies

and **bows**.

Mrs. Howard plays a butterfly tune on the piano and we **flutter** and **float** and **flap** our butterfly wings.

Then the music changes.
Thump! Crash! Whump!
It's a dinosaur song! We all
stamp and clomp in time to it.
Jake loves being a dinosaur!

We do leg bends and jumps next. Miss Anne calls
them **pliés** and **jetés**.

That's leg bends and jumps in French.

When our moms and dads come
to pick us up, Miss Anne says:
"Remember to practice your own dances
for the show next week, please."

I practice my part every single day.
I want to be just like a real cat:

a leapy cat,

a curled-up-to-sleepy cat,

a stretchy cat,

a pounce-on-a-mousey cat.

I can't wait for the show on Tuesday.

On the day of the show,
everyone's excited.
We all change into our
special costumes. I have a long,
velvety tail and ears, and Mom draws
whiskers on my cheeks with face paint.

My tummy feels funny.
Mom says it's full of
butterflies because
I'm a little nervous.

The music starts and we all run onto the stage. I swish my tail. First, I'm a tiptoe-on-my-paws cat, and then I'm a fierce show-all-my-claws cat.

I'm the most perfect cat I can be. Jake is a growly bear and Katie swoops around the stage like a bluebird.

When the show is over, everyone claps very loudly and we do our best curtsies and bows. I wave at my mom and dad.

Miss Anne tells us we all danced beautifully. Mom says my dance was lovely. Dad says he thought I was a real cat.

I say, "Meow!" which means thank you!

Now I can't wait for next Tuesday. I LOVE ballet!